For Balder

Copyright © 2022 Clavis Publishing Inc., New York

Originally published as *Hop op zwemles* in Belgium and the Netherlands by Clavis Uitgeverij, 2021
English translation from the Dutch by Clavis Publishing Inc., New York

Visit us on the Web at www.clavis-publishing.com.

Hop at Swimming Class written and illustrated by Esther van den Berg

ISBN 978-1-60537-734-6

This book was printed in February 2022 at Nikara,
M. R. Štefánika 858/25, 963 01 Krupina, Slovakia.

First Edition
10 9 8 7 6 5 4 3 2 1

Clavis Publishing supports the First Amendment and celebrates the right to read.

Esther van den Berg

Hop at Swimming Class

Clavis
NEW YORK

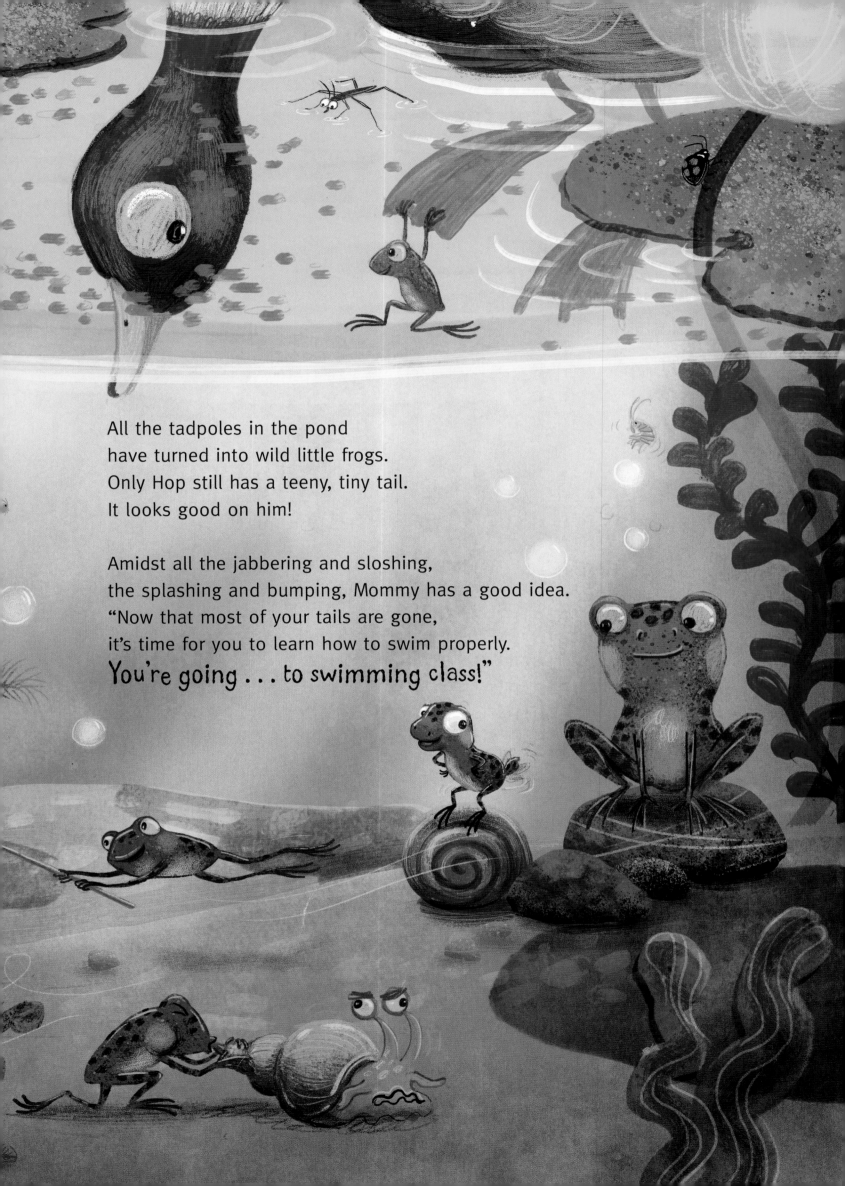

All the tadpoles in the pond
have turned into wild little frogs.
Only Hop still has a teeny, tiny tail.
It looks good on him!

Amidst all the jabbering and sloshing,
the splashing and bumping, Mommy has a good idea.
"Now that most of your tails are gone,
it's time for you to learn how to swim properly.
You're going . . . to swimming class!"

All the frogs put on their floaties.

Hop's front legs are still a little too short.
Only his fingertips stick out, but he's sure to stay afloat!

There's Lifeguard Toad.
"You may call me Toadguard."

Toadguard looks stern, but then he sees Hop.
When he smiles, he looks kind.
He helps Hop into a lifesaver, which fits better.
"Hup, Hop! Let's get started!"

"First we learn how to float."
Taking turns, the little frogs float on their backs,
with their bellies up.

"Almost right, Hop.
Now the other
way around."

Hop twists and turns in the water.
"Easy, Hop! Slow and steady,"
says Toadguard.

"Yes, like that!"
Hop still wobbles a little,
but he floats!

"Now we'll learn how to tread water."

First the little frogs practice with floaties . . .

. . . and then without.
Hop goes under.
"Keep on kicking!" Toadguard roars.

Hop comes back up, coughing, but he's still kicking!

"Leave the floaties and follow me. Backstroke to the other side." Toadguard leads the way, and a neat string of little frogs follows.

Hop goes the wrong way, but he finds a beautiful butterfly!

Toadguard unties Hop and practices with him one more time.
"Frog. Airplane. Pencil." There he goes!

Hop doesn't go very fast, but he reaches the other side!

"And now my favorite part!"
Toadguard poses perkily in his suit.
"Swimming with clothes on!"

A witch, a tiger, and a pirate are
the first ones to reach the other side.

Hop arrives last,
but he puts on a great show!

What fun!
And only one more part to go
before getting their swimming diplomas . . .

"A frog makes beautiful leaps.
Let's see how beautifully you can jump."
Hop chooses the lowest diving board.

How strange,
his diving board
goes up . . .

. . . and up . . .

. . . and up . . .

Uh-oh...

Hop dives off the highest diving board
and does the coolest frog jump!
It happened by accident,
but it was quite brave.

"A brave frog like you deserves
a swimming diploma!"
Toadguard says.
"Great job, Hop! Well done!"

Now that all the little frogs
have learned how to swim,
peace has returned to the pond.

But for how long?

Not that long . . .

"CANNONBALL!"